Fern the Green Fairy

*To the fairies at the
bottom of my garden*

*Special thanks to
Narinder Dhani*

No part of this publication may be reproduced or
stored in a retrieval system, or transmitted in any
form or by any means, electronic, mechanical,
photocopying, recording, or otherwise, without
written permission of the publisher. For information
regarding permission, write to Working Partners Limited,
1 Albion Place, London W6 OQT.

ISBN 0-439-69191-5

12   8 9 10/0

Printed in the U.S.A.

First Scholastic printing, February 2005

Fern the Green Fairy

by Daisy Meadows
illustrated by Georgie Ripper

SCHOLASTIC INC.

New York   Toronto   London   Auckland   Sydney
Mexico City   New Delhi   Hong Kong   Buenos Aires

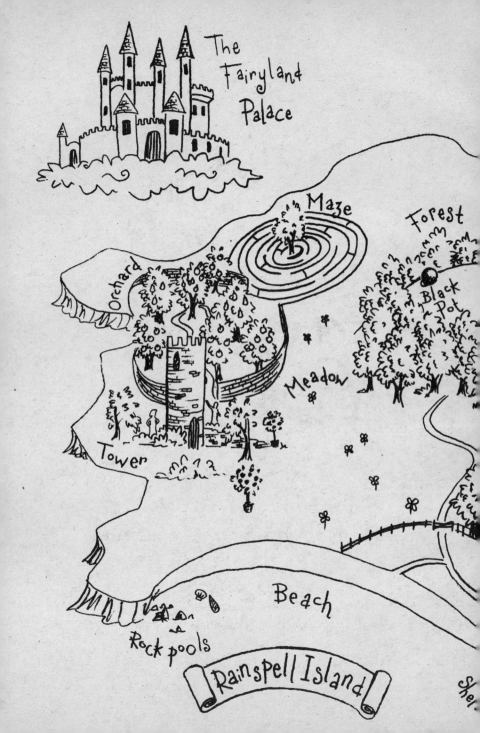

Cold winds blow and thick ice forms,
I conjure up this fairy storm.
To seven corners of the mortal world
the Rainbow Fairies will be hurled!

I curse every part of Fairyland,
with a frosty wave of my icy hand.
For now and always, from this fateful day,
Fairyland will be cold and gray!

Ruby, Amber, and Saffron
are out of danger.
Will Rachel and Kirsty free
Fern the Green Fairy, too?

Contents

The Secret Garden

The Secret Garden

"Oh!" Rachel Walker gasped in delight as she gazed around her. "What a perfect place for a picnic!"

"It's a secret garden," Kirsty Tate said, her eyes shining.

They were standing in a large garden. It looked as if nobody else had been there for a long, long time. Pink and white roses grew all around the tree trunks, filling the air with sweet perfume. White marble statues stood here and there, half hidden by trailing, green ivy. And right in the middle of the garden was a crumbling stone tower.

"There was a castle here once called Moonspinner Castle," Mr. Walker said, looking at his guidebook. "But now all that's left is the tower."

Rachel and Kirsty stared up at the ruined tower. The yellow stones glowed warmly in the sunshine. They were covered in soft, green moss. Near the top of the tower was a small, square window.

"It's just like Rapunzel's tower," Kirsty said. "I wonder if we can get up to the top?"

"Let's go see!" Rachel said eagerly. "I want to explore the whole garden. Can we, Mom?"

"Go ahead." Mrs. Walker smiled. "Your dad and I will get the food ready." She opened the picnic basket. "But don't be too long, girls."

Rachel and Kirsty rushed over to the door in the side of the tower. Kirsty tugged at the heavy iron handle. But the door was locked.

Rachel felt disappointed. "Oh, that's too bad," she said.

Kirsty sighed. "Yes, I was hoping Fern the Green Fairy might be here."

Rachel and Kirsty had a secret. They were helping to find the seven Rainbow Fairies before the end of their vacation on Rainspell Island. The fairies had been cast out of Fairyland by evil Jack Frost, and Fairyland had lost all its color. Only when all seven fairies returned home would Fairyland be bright and beautiful again.

"Fern," Rachel called in a low voice. "Are you here?"

Here . . . Here . . . Here . . .

Her words echoed off the stones. Rachel and Kirsty held their breath and waited. But they couldn't hear anything except leaves rustling in the breeze.

"It's such a special place," Kirsty said.

"It *feels* like there's magic close by." Then she gasped and pointed. "Rachel, look at the ivy!"

Rachel stared. Glossy green leaves grew thickly on the wall, but in one place the stones were bare, in the shape of a perfect circle.

Rachel's heart began to beat faster. "It's

just like a fairy ring!" she said. She ran around the tower to take a closer look and almost tripped over the lace of one of her sneakers.

"Careful!" Kirsty said, grabbing Rachel's arm.

Rachel sat down on a mossy stone to retie her shoelace. "There's green *everywhere*," she said, looking around at the lush grass and the leafy trees. "Fern *must* be here."

"We'd better find her quickly, then," Kirsty said with a shiver. "In case Jack Frost's goblins find her first!"

Jack Frost had sent his goblin servants to Rainspell. He wanted them to stop the fairies from getting home to Fairyland.

"Where should we start looking?" Rachel asked, standing up again.

Kirsty laughed. "You've got green stuff all over you!" she said.

Rachel twisted around to look. The back of her denim skirt was green and dusty. "It must be the moss," she grumbled, brushing it off.

The dust flew up into the air. It sparkled and glittered in the morning sun. As it fell to the ground, tiny green leaves appeared and the smell of freshly cut grass filled the air.

Rachel and Kirsty turned to each other. "It's fairy dust!" they cried together.

Where Is Fern?

"Fern *is* here!" said Kirsty.

"Thank goodness I sat down on that fairy dust!" Rachel said.

They walked all around the tower, looking under bushes and inside sweet-smelling flowers. As they walked, they softly called Fern's name. But the Green Fairy was nowhere to be found.

"You don't think the goblins have caught her, do you?" Rachel said, feeling very worried.

"I hope not," replied Kirsty. "I'm sure Fern *was* here, but now she's somewhere else."

"Yes, but where?" Rachel looked around the garden in despair.

"Maybe there's magic around to help us," Kirsty said hopefully.

She looked down at the tiny leaves. Some of them had begun to flutter across the garden. "I know, let's follow the fairy dust."

The bright green leaves floated over to a narrow path that led into a beautiful orchard. Rachel could see apples, pears, and plums growing on the trees.

"It's a magic trail!" Kirsty breathed.

"Quick, let's keep following the fairy dust," Rachel said.

Rachel and Kirsty set off along the path, which twisted and turned through the fruit trees.

Suddenly, the path opened out into a large clearing. Kirsty's eyes opened wide when she saw what was in front of them. "It's a maze!" she cried.

The thick, green hedges loomed above them, their leaves rustling softly.

Rachel nudged Kirsty. "Look." She pointed. "The fairy trail goes right into the maze!"

"We'll have to follow it," Kirsty said
bravely.

The two girls followed the floating
fairy leaves through the narrow
entrance. Kirsty felt a bit scared as the
fairy dust led them first one way, then
another, between the green hedges.
What if the trail ran out and they got
lost in the maze?

"Maybe there'll be another clue in the middle of the maze," Rachel said hopefully.

"Or maybe Fern will be there!" Kirsty added.

They turned one more corner and, suddenly, the hedges parted to reveal the center of the maze. An oak tree stood in the very middle. The fairy dust led right to the bottom of the tree, then stopped. "Fern must be here!" Rachel said excitedly.

Kirsty frowned. "Yes, but *where*?" she asked, looking around.

Tap! Tap! Tap!

The two girls jumped.

"What was that?" Rachel gasped.

There it was again. *Tap! Tap! Tap!*

Kirsty's eyes opened wide. "It's coming from over there." She pointed at the oak tree.

"I hope it isn't a goblin trap," Rachel whispered.

Tap! Tap! Tap!

The noise was louder now. Slowly, Rachel and Kirsty walked right around the tree. At first they couldn't see anything unusual.

Then Rachel pointed at the trunk. "What's a *window* doing in a *tree*?" She gasped.

There was a small, hollow knot halfway up the trunk — and it was covered by a glass window!

Kirsty put out her hand and touched the window. It was very cold and wet. "It's not glass," she whispered. "It's *ice*!"

Both girls looked more closely. Suddenly, something moved behind the icy window. Kirsty could just make out a tiny girl dressed in glittering green.

"Rachel, we've found her!" she said happily. "It's Fern the Green Fairy!"

Lost in the Maze

Fern waved to the girls through the sheet of ice. Her mouth opened and closed, but Rachel and Kirsty couldn't hear a word she was saying. The ice was too thick.

Rachel looked worried. "She must be freezing in there," she said. "We've got to get her out."

"We could smash the ice with a stick," said Kirsty. Then she frowned. "But Fern might get hurt."

Rachel thought hard. "We could *melt* the ice," she said.

"How?" Kirsty asked.

"Like this," Rachel replied. She reached up and pressed her hand firmly against the window of ice. Kirsty did the same. The ice felt freezing cold, but they kept on pressing against it with their warm hands.

Soon, a few drops of water began to trickle down the window.

"It's melting!" Rachel said. "We can make a hole in it now." She gently poked the middle of the window with her finger, and the ice began to crack.

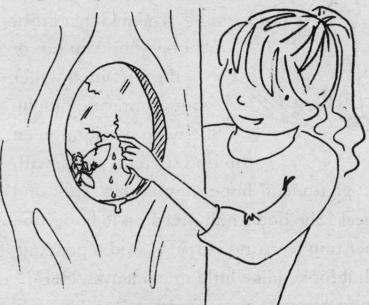

"Don't worry, Fern," cried Kirsty. "You'll be out of there very soon!"

There was a sudden crack as the ice split open. A flash of sparkling fairy dust shot out, leaving behind a lovely scent of cut grass. And then Fern the Green Fairy pushed her way out of the icy window, her wings fluttering limply. She wore a bright green top and stretchy pants, with pretty leaf shapes around her waist and neck. She had small green pixie boots on her tiny feet, and earrings, and a pendant that looked like little green leaves. Her long, brown hair was tied in bunches, and her slender, emerald wand was tipped with gold.

"Oh, I'm s-s-so c-c-cold!" the fairy gasped, shivering all over. She floated down to rest on Kirsty's shoulder.

"Let me warm you up a bit," said Rachel. She scooped the fairy up and held her in her cupped hands. Then she blew gently on her.

The warmth of Rachel's breath seemed to do the trick. Fern stopped shivering, and her wings straightened out. "Thank you," she said. "I feel much better now."

"I'm Rachel and this is Kirsty," Rachel explained. "We're here to take you to the pot-at-the-end-of-the-rainbow."

"Ruby, Amber, and Saffron are waiting for you," Kirsty added. Fern's green eyes lit up. "They're safe!" she exclaimed. "That's wonderful!" She flew off Rachel's hand in a blaze of green fairy dust and twirled

joyfully in the air. "But what about my other sisters?"

"Don't worry, we're going to find them, too," Kirsty told her. "How did you get stuck behind the ice window?"

"When I landed on Rainspell Island, I got tangled up in the ivy on the tower," Fern explained. "I managed to untangle myself, but then Jack Frost's goblins started chasing me. So I ran into the maze and hid in the oak tree. But it was raining, and when the goblins passed by, the rainwater turned to ice. So I was trapped."

Suddenly, Rachel shivered. "It's getting colder," she said. She glanced up at the sky. The sun had disappeared behind a cloud, and there was a sudden chill in the air.

"The goblins must be close by!" Kirsty gasped, looking scared.

Fern nodded. "Yes, we'd better get out of this garden right away," she said calmly. "You know the way, don't you?"

Rachel and Kirsty looked at each other.

"I'm not sure," Kirsty said with a frown. "Do *you* know, Rachel?"

Rachel shook her head. "No," she replied. "But we can follow the fairy trail back to the start of the maze."

Kirsty looked around. "Where *is* the fairy trail?" she asked.

An icy breeze was blowing all around them now. The green fairy leaves were drifting away and vanishing in front of their very eyes.

"Oh, no!" Kirsty cried. "What are we going to do now?"

Suddenly, they heard the sound of heavy footsteps coming through the maze toward them.

"I know that fairy is in here *somewhere*," grumbled a loud, gruff voice.

Fern, Rachel, and Kirsty stared at one another in dismay.

"Goblins!" whispered Rachel.

Fairy Fireworks

Rachel, Kirsty, and Fern listened in horror as the goblins came closer. As usual, they were arguing with each other.

"Come on!" snorted one goblin. "We can't let her get away again."

"Stop bossing me around," whined the other one. "I'm going as fast as I can. OW!"

There was a loud *THUD!* It sounded as if the goblin had fallen over.

"If your feet weren't so big, you wouldn't trip over them," jeered the first goblin.

"They're big enough to give you a good kick!" the other goblin snapped.

"Let's hide in the tree," Fern whispered to Rachel and Kirsty. "I'll make you fairy-sized so we can all fit under a leaf." Quickly, she shot up into the air and sprinkled the girls with fairy dust. Rachel and Kirsty gasped as they felt themselves shrinking, down and down. It was so exciting! Fern took the girls' hands. "Let's go," she

said, and the three of them fluttered up
into the air and landed on a branch. Fat
brown acorns grew on the tree, as big as

beach balls. Even the thinnest twigs
looked like tree trunks to the tiny girls!
Fern heaved up the edge of a leaf, which
was as big as a tablecloth, and they all
crept underneath.

A moment later, the goblins rushed into the clearing.

"Where can that fairy be?" grumbled one of them. "I know she came this way!"

They began to search around the bottom of the tree.

"How are we going to get back to the pot?" Rachel whispered to Fern.

Fern laughed. "Don't worry! I think I know someone who can help us!" And she pointed past them.

Rachel and Kirsty turned to look.
A furry, gray face was peeping shyly
around the tree trunk. It was a squirrel.

"Hello," Fern called softly.

The squirrel jumped and hid behind the
trunk. Then he peeped out again, his dark
eyes curious.

"Maybe he'd like an acorn." Kirsty
suggested.

There was a big, shiny nut growing
right next to her. She wrapped
her arms around it, but she
couldn't pull it off the
twig. Rachel and Fern
came to help. All
three of them tugged
at the acorn until it
came off the branch with
a jump.

Fern held it out to the squirrel. "Mmm, a yummy nut!" she said.

The squirrel ran lightly along the branch, his long, furry tail waving. He took the acorn and held it in his front paws.

"What's your name?" asked Fern kindly.

"I'm Fluffy," squeaked the squirrel, between nibbles.

"I'm Fern," said the fairy. "And these are my friends Rachel and Kirsty. We need to get away from the goblins. Will you help us?"

Fluffy shivered. "I don't like goblins," he squeaked.

"We won't let them hurt you," Fern promised, stroking his head. "Can you give us a ride on your back? You can jump from hedge to hedge much better than we can! We have to get out of the maze."

"Yes, I'll help you," Fluffy agreed, finishing the last piece of acorn.

Rachel, Kirsty, and Fern climbed onto the squirrel's back. Kirsty thought it was just like sinking into a big, soft blanket.

"This is great," said Fern, snuggling down into the squirrel's fur. "Let's go, Fluffy!"

The squirrel turned and ran along the branch. Rachel, Kirsty, and Fern clung tightly to Fluffy's thick fur as he jumped out of the tree, right over the goblins' heads! He landed neatly on the nearest

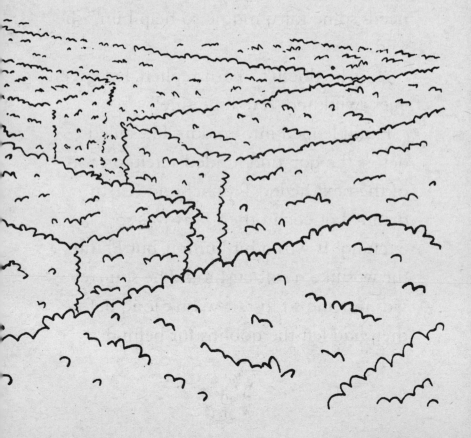

hedge. The goblins were so busy arguing, they didn't even notice.

Fern leaned forward to whisper in the squirrel's ear. "Well done, Fluffy. Now, the next one!"

Rachel gulped when she saw how far away the next hedge was. "Maybe Fluffy needs some fairy magic to help him," she said.

"No, he doesn't," Fern replied, her green eyes twinkling. "He'll be fine!"

Fluffy leaped into midair. He sailed across the gap and landed safely on top of the next hedge. Rachel and Kirsty grinned at each other. This was so exciting! It was a bit bumpy, but Fluffy's fur was like a soft cushion. The squirrel was moving so fast, it wasn't long before they had left the goblins far behind.

"Here we are," Fern said at last, as Fluffy reached the edge of the maze. "Now, which way do we go, girls?"

Rachel and Kirsty looked at each other in dismay. "This isn't the way we came *in*," Rachel said. "And I don't know the way back to the pot. Do you, Kirsty?"

Kirsty shook her head.

Fern looked worried. "But I have to get back to the pot!" she said.

"Oh!" Kirsty had an idea. "Rachel, what about looking in our magic bags?"

"Good idea," Rachel agreed.

Titania, the Fairy Queen, had given Rachel and Kirsty two special magic bags, for whenever they needed help.

The girls took the bags with them everywhere.

Fluffy scrambled down the hedge to the ground, and Rachel, Kirsty, and Fern climbed off his back. Kirsty opened her backpack and looked inside. One of the magic bags was glowing with a silvery light. "I wonder what's inside," she said, reaching in.

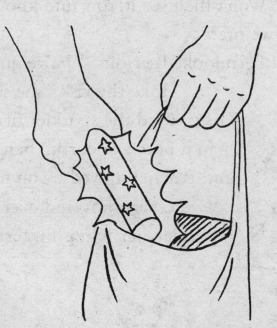

She pulled out a thin, green stick covered with sparkling gold stars.

"It looks like a *sparkler*," Rachel said. "That's not much use, is it?"

"It's a fairy sparkler!" said Fern excitedly. "We can shoot it into the sky, and my sisters will see it from the pot. Then they'll know we need help."

"But what about the goblins?" Rachel asked. "Won't they see it, too, and know where we are?"

Fern looked serious. "We've got to take the risk," she said. Kirsty stood the sparkler firmly in a patch of earth, then she and Rachel moved away from it. Fern hovered over the sparkler, her wings fluttering.

She touched the top with her wand and quickly flew back to the girls.

Rachel and Kirsty held their breath as the tube caught light. Suddenly, with a loud fizz, the sparkler shot upward, trailing bright green sparks behind it. It climbed higher and higher into the sky, until it burst into a shower of emerald stars. The stars spelled out the words

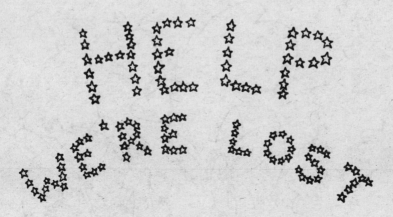

They twinkled brightly in the
darkening sky before fading away.

"We won't have to wait long," Fern
said. "Help will come very soon."

Rachel and Kirsty wondered what was
going to happen. How could the fairies
come to their rescue? They weren't
supposed to leave the clearing where the
pot was, in case the goblins found them.

Suddenly, there was a rustle of leaves behind them.

"Did you see the fairy sparkler?" shouted a loud voice. "It came from over there. Quick, before that fairy gets away again!"

Hedgehog Help

Rachel and Kirsty stared at each other in alarm. Fluffy looked scared, too. The goblins were on their trail again!

"They're coming toward us," Rachel whispered as the voices got louder.

"Don't worry," Fern said, smiling. "My sisters will send help quickly."

Then Rachel spotted a line of golden sparkles twinkling toward them through the fruit trees. "What's that?" she whispered.

"Is it goblin magic?" Kirsty asked anxiously.

Fern shook her head. "They're fireflies! My sisters must have sent them to show us the way back to the pot."

Suddenly, there was another shout from inside the maze. "Look, what are those lights over there?"

"The goblins have spotted the fireflies!" Rachel gasped.

"Quickly, Fluffy!" Fern said as they climbed onto the squirrel's back again. "Follow the fireflies!"

The golden specks were dancing away through the trees. Fluffy scampered after them, just as the goblins dashed out of the maze.

"There's the fairy!" one of them shouted, pointing at Fern. "Stop that squirrel!"

"Come back!" the other roared as Fluffy ran off.

Rachel, Kirsty, and Fern clung to Fluffy's fur as the squirrel zigzagged this way and that to get away from the goblins. Fluffy scrambled up the trunk of the nearest tree. He was just about to jump across to the next, when someone called to them from below.

"Hello!"

"Who's that?" Rachel asked. She, Kirsty, and Fern peered down at the ground. A hedgehog was standing at the foot of the apple tree. "Hello!" he called again. "The

52

animals in the garden have heard that you're in trouble. We'd like to help."

"Oh, thank you!" Fern called. Then she gasped as the two goblins appeared among the trees.

"Where'd that squirrel go?" one of them yelled.

Quickly, Fluffy leaped across to the next apple tree. The goblins roared with rage and dashed forward. At that very moment, the hedgehog curled himself into a ball and rolled right into their path. Rachel thought he looked like a big, prickly football.

"OW!" both goblins howled. "My toes!"

Rachel and Kirsty couldn't help laughing as the goblins jumped around holding their feet. "Hooray for Hedgehog!" they shouted.

As Fluffy jumped from one fruit tree to the next, the firefly lights behind them began to go out.

"Hey! Who turned off the lights?" wailed one of the goblins, still rubbing his foot. "Which way are we supposed to go?"

"How do I know?" snapped the other goblin. Their voices were getting fainter now as Fluffy hurried on.

"Thank you, fireflies!" called Fern, waving at the last few specks of light. "Now, we need to find a way to the orchard wall. We can't be far from the pot now."

"I can help you," a small voice
whispered.

A fawn was standing at the bottom of
the tree. Her golden brown
coat was short and
silky, and she stared
up at them with big,
brown eyes.

"You mean you
can show us the
way?" Kirsty said.

"Yes, I can." The deer
nodded, twitching her little
tail. "I can show you a shortcut."
She trotted off through the trees on her
long legs. Fluffy followed her, leaping
from branch to branch above the little
deer's head.

Rachel was so excited she could hardly

breathe. She was riding on a squirrel's
back, being shown the way to the pot-at-
the-end-of-the-rainbow by a fawn!

A few moments later, they reached the
brick wall that ran around the outside of
the orchard. Fluffy leaped up to the top
of the wall, and Rachel and Kirsty
looked eagerly ahead of them. On the
other side of the wall was a meadow, and
beyond that woods.

"Look!" Rachel shouted. "That's where
the pot is!"

Flying High

"Thank you!" Kirsty and Rachel called
to the baby deer. She blinked her long
eyelashes at them and trotted away.

A blackbird with shiny, dark feathers
was sitting on the wall a little way away.
He hopped over to them, his head on one
side. "I'm here to take you to the pot-at-

the-end-of-the-rainbow," he chirped. "All aboard!"

Fluffy looked sad as Fern, Rachel, and Kirsty slid off his back and climbed onto the blackbird. It was a tight squeeze, and the feathers felt smooth and silky after Fluffy's fur.

"Good-bye, Fluffy!" called Rachel, and she blew him a kiss. She felt sad to leave

their new friend behind. The blackbird
soared into the air.

"Look for the big weeping willow tree,"
Rachel told the blackbird as he swooped
across the meadow.

"I can't wait to see my sisters again,"
said Fern, sounding very excited.

The blackbird flew over the woods and
landed in the clearing near the willow

tree. Rachel, Kirsty, and Fern jumped
down onto the grass.

"Who's there?" croaked a stern voice. A
plump, green frog hopped out
from under the hanging
branches of the tree.
"Bertram, it's me!" Fern
called. Quickly, the fairy
waved her wand, and Rachel
and Kirsty shot up to their
normal size again.

"Miss Fern!" Bertram said joyfully.
"You're back!"

"We followed the fireflies," Fern said,
giving the frog a hug. "Thank you for
sending them."

"We saw the sparkler in the sky,"
Bertram explained, "so we knew you
were in trouble. But you'll be safe here,"

he went on. "The pot is hidden under the tree."

Rachel and Kirsty hurried over and pulled aside the long branches. The pot-at-the-end-of-the-rainbow lay there on its side.

Suddenly, a fountain of red, orange, and yellow fairy dust whooshed out of the pot. Ruby, Amber, and Saffron flew out, looking very excited. A big queen bee buzzed out behind them.

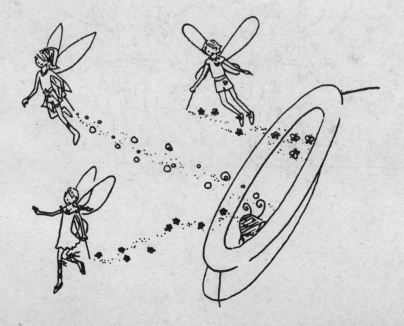

"Fern!" Ruby called. "You're safe! It's so good to see you!"

Rachel and Kirsty beamed as they watched the fairies hug each other. The air around them fizzed and popped with red flowers, green leaves, tiny yellow butterflies, and orange bubbles.

"We really missed you," said Saffron.
Beside her, the bee nudged her with a
tiny feeler. "Oh, sorry, Queenie," said
Saffron. "This is my sister Fern."

Queenie buzzed, "Hello!"

"How did you get back so
quickly?" asked Amber. "We sent
the fireflies only a little
while ago."

"Our woodland friends
helped us," Fern said. She
waved as the blackbird flew
off. "Especially Fluffy the
squirrel." She sighed. "It was a
shame we had to leave him
behind."

Ruby laughed. "Who's that, then?" she
asked, pointing at a tree on the other side
of the clearing.

Rachel and Kirsty looked, too. Fluffy was peeping at them from behind the tree trunk, looking very shy.

"Fluffy!" Fern flew over and hugged him. "What are you doing here?"

"I was worried about you," Fluffy explained shyly. "I wanted to make sure you got back to the pot safely."

"Would you like to stay with us, too?" asked Amber. "You could live in the willow tree, couldn't you?"

"Yes, *please*," squeaked Fluffy.

Ruby turned to Rachel and Kirsty. "Thank you again," she said. "I don't know what we'd do without you!"

Fern fluttered lightly onto Rachel's shoulder. One of her wings brushed softly against Rachel's cheek, like a butterfly. "We'll see you again soon, won't we?"

"Yes, of course," Rachel promised.

"Only three more Rainbow Fairies left to find!" Kirsty added. She took Rachel's hand and they waved to the fairies, before running out of the clearing. "We'd better get back to your mom and dad, Rachel. They'll be wondering where we are."

"Good idea." Rachel laughed. "We'd better hurry back, before my dad eats all the picnic!"

RAINBOW magic

Ruby, Amber, Saffron, and Fern have been found. Now Rachel and Kirsty must seek out

Sky the Blue Fairy

A Magic Messenger

"The water's really warm!" Rachel
Walker laughed. She was sitting on a
rock, swishing her toes in one of
Rainspell Island's deep blue rock pools.
Her friend Kirsty Tate was looking for
shells on the rocks nearby.

"Be careful you don't slip, Kirsty!"

called Mrs. Tate. She was sitting farther down the beach with Mrs. Walker.

"OK, Mom!" Kirsty yelled back. As she looked down at her bare feet, a patch of green seaweed began to move. There was something blue and shiny underneath it. "Rachel! Come over here," she shouted.

Rachel went over to Kirsty. "What is it?" she asked.

Kirsty pointed to the seaweed.

"There's something blue under there," she said. "I wonder, could it be . . ."

"Sky the Blue Fairy?" Rachel said eagerly.

Jack Frost had banished the seven Rainbow Fairies from Fairyland with a magic spell. Now they were hidden on Rainspell Island. Until they were all found there would be no color in

Fairyland. Rachel and Kirsty had promised the Fairy King and Queen to help find them.

The seaweed twitched.

Rachel felt her heart beat faster.

Read the rest of

Sky the Blue Fairy

to find out what magic
is hiding in the shiny seaweed.